For Daniel and the ba, from your Granja

This edition published by Parragon Books Ltd in 2015 and distributed by

Parragon Inc.
440 Park Avenue South, 13th Floor
New York, NY 10016
www.parragon.com

Written by Malachy Doyle   Illustrated by Barroux
Edited by Laura Baker and Grace Harvey   Designed by Karissa Santos
Production by Emma Fulleylove

ISBN 978-1-4723-7897-2

Printed in China

The NOSe THAT KNOWS

PaRragon

Bath • New York • Cologne • Melbourne • Delhi
Hong Kong • Shenzhen • Singapore • Amsterdam

Milo loves his owner.
She's a girl called Molly Brown.

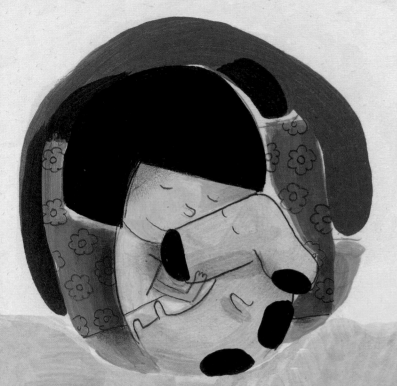

But Milo's nose loves
food the most ...

It leads him all round town.

For Milo's nose is a nose
that knows—it knows
when food is near.

When it smells a smell,
the nose soon shows
poor Milo where to steer!

Molly's heading out with Mom.
Milo runs. **BARK! BARK!**

But the nose
has sniffed a
SANDWICH
moving quickly
through the park!

Where that nose goes, Milo goes ...

SPLASH! So now he's paddling through a pond!

Then his nose smells a smell
of which he's really rather fond!

It's coming from that office block.

Oh my—it does smell fine!

The nose has caught a sniff of cheese
and pies and fries—**WHERE'S MINE?**

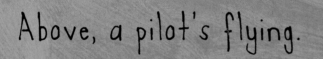

Above, a pilot's flying.

Is that **PIZZA** on a plate?

The nose that knows
drags Milo, but—
OH NO!—
he's just too late!

He clings on to the 'copter
as it flies off through the air ...

But then his nose smells ...

... crunchy, munchy **APPLES** over there!

They're in that
massive rocket—
he'll just grab one,
then he'll go.

He sneaks in,
but the doors close ...

SIX

FIVE

FOUR

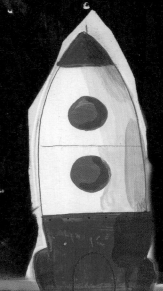

Out he climbs,
and finds the
moon is made of

PEANUT
BUTTER!

He tries to lick,
but then his nose
smells something
oh so nice!

It's miles and
miles away, but
it smells just
like paradise!

His nose, it knows what's cooking—
it's his favorite thing to eat ...
Cooking on a barbecue, it's yummy,
sizzling **MEAT!**

"Hey! You're back!" cries Molly.
"Wherever did you go?"
Milo wags his tail, but
she will never ever know!

Molly is just glad he's home and gives him
ONE HUGE TREAT!

Milo's glad to be back, too,
and glad—at last—to eat.

So Milo, he might wander.
Yes Milo, he might roam.
But Milo's nose is a nose that knows
and will always lead him to ...

MOLLY, FOOD, and HOME!